Adia R.

THIS BOOK BELONGS TO

ADIA

children's choice®

Professor Noah's Spaceship

Professor Noah's Spaceship

BRIAN WILDSMITH

Oxford University Press 1980   OXFORD   NEW YORK   TORONTO   MELBOURNE

Printed in USA

ISBN: 0-590-75814-4

Once upon a time there was a huge forest,

and all kinds of animals and birds lived happily there.

As the years passed,
the forest began
to change.
The air around it
started to smell
and turned a nasty
color.
No longer did the
sunlight filter
joyfully through
the leaves.
The leaves
started to fall
from the trees,
and their fruit
began to turn bad.

A strange sadness came over the forest.
The animals and birds were bewildered.
'What's happening to our forest?'
they all cried.
They became so desperate that Lion,
the king of beasts, decided to call
a meeting of all animals and birds.
'It is clear that we are in
grave danger,' roared Lion.
'Our forest is being destroyed
and very soon we shall have
no place to live and no food
to eat.'

'The air is so foul that when I run I get out
of breath,' growled Coati.
'The bananas aren't fit to eat,' chattered Monkey.
'The oranges are terrible,' bellowed Elephant.

'When I sit on my eggs to hatch them, they break,'
piped Pelican.
Lion sighed. 'My friends, we must do something.
Our very lives are in peril.
Does anyone have an idea what we should do?'

'Owl, you are the wise one among us,' said Lion.
'What must we do?'
'During my flights over the forest,' said Owl,
'I have observed a huge and wondrous object being built.
Whoever is building this must be very clever.
He should be able to tell us what to do.
We must go there at once. Follow me.'

They arrived at a huge fence surrounding
a strange object.
'I must see what is going on,' said Lion.
'Elephant, lift me up so that I can see
over the fence.' And so, Elephant lifted him up.
'Extraordinary! My, my, how very extraordinary!'
said Lion. 'I have never seen anything like it.
Whoever is building this must be very clever indeed.
We must go in and see him.'

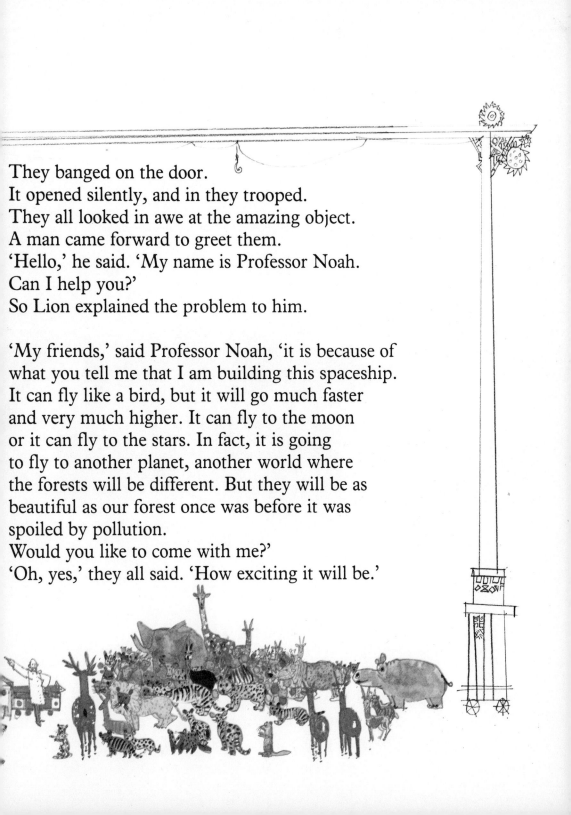

They banged on the door.
It opened silently, and in they trooped.
They all looked in awe at the amazing object.
A man came forward to greet them.
'Hello,' he said. 'My name is Professor Noah.
Can I help you?'
So Lion explained the problem to him.

'My friends,' said Professor Noah, 'it is because of
what you tell me that I am building this spaceship.
It can fly like a bird, but it will go much faster
and very much higher. It can fly to the moon
or it can fly to the stars. In fact, it is going
to fly to another planet, another world where
the forests will be different. But they will be as
beautiful as our forest once was before it was
spoiled by pollution.
Would you like to come with me?'
'Oh, yes,' they all said. 'How exciting it will be.'

'The spaceship will soon be finished,'
said Professor Noah. 'My robots do most of the work,
but I could do with a little help.'
And so the animals helped, as much as they could.
When the spaceship was nearly finished, they all
had a very good time, playing with the robots.

One day Professor Noah announced,
'My friends, we have not much time left.
There is still work to be done.
We shall need food for each of you,
as our journey will last forty days and forty nights.'
All the animals brought food and loaded it on
the spaceship.

When the work was almost finished, Owl came flying in
from one of his trips around the forest, and cried in fear,
'The forest is on fire. They are not only polluting it—
now they are burning it.'

'Hurry,' cried Professor Noah.
'We must finish the work quickly.'
When all was ready, they boarded the spaceship.

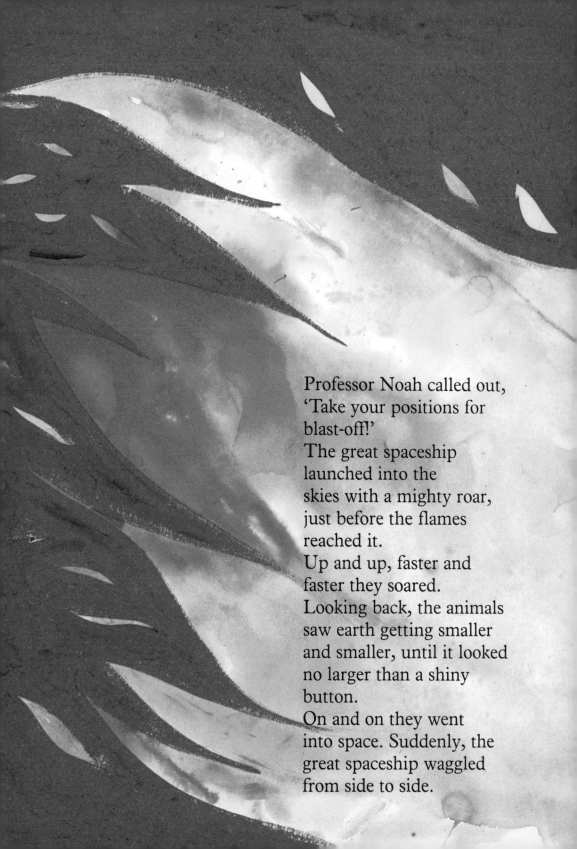

Professor Noah called out,
'Take your positions for
blast-off!'
The great spaceship
launched into the
skies with a mighty roar,
just before the flames
reached it.
Up and up, faster and
faster they soared.
Looking back, the animals
saw earth getting smaller
and smaller, until it looked
no larger than a shiny
button.
On and on they went
into space. Suddenly, the
great spaceship waggled
from side to side.

'Oh dear,'
said Professor Noah.
'One of our time guidance
fins has been damaged
on take-off. It must be
in the correct position to
take us hundreds of years
into the future and help us
reach our new planet.
I need a strong volunteer
to go into space and twist
the fin back into shape.'
'I'll go,' said Elephant.
He put on a special
space-suit, went out
through the air-lock,
and pulled the fin into shape.
'Hurray!' they all shouted.
Professor Noah gave him
ten oranges and called
him a hero.

They traveled through space
for forty days and forty nights.
The further they went,
the sadder the animals became.
'I'm so homesick,' said Gnu.
'Me, too,' cried Llama.
'We're all homesick,' everyone wailed.
'Oh dear, oh dear,'
said Professor Noah.

At last they approached their
new planet. 'I must make sure
all is well for us there,'
said Professor Noah.
'Dove, go out and bring
back a leaf from a tree.'
Dove did as he was told
and came back with a leaf.

Professor Noah tested it in his computer.
'Why, I can't believe it,' he cried. 'It is most
extraordinary. This is a leaf from planet Earth.
I must check my calculations.'
After making many checks, he called a meeting.
'My friends,' he said, 'when Elephant tried
to repair our time guidance system, he must
have twisted it the wrong way.

We have traveled *backwards* through time,
back to planet Earth as it was many hundreds
of years ago, before it was polluted.'
'Hurray!' they all cheered.
'Does this mean that we have come back to Earth
as it was in the beginning?' said Lion.
'Yes,' said Professor Noah. 'It is a wonderful world,
and we must keep it that way.'

As the sun rose,
the spaceship
descended
to Earth.
'How lovely it is,'
the animals cried.
They all thanked
Professor Noah
for saving them.
And then they left
joyfully for their
new home.

'I think it's been raining,' said Otter, splashing in a blue puddle.
'There seems to have been some flooding here.'